Brenda
the Bold

Jean Ure

Illustrated by
GLENYS AMBRUS

HEINEMANN · LONDON

William Heinemann Ltd
10 Upper Grosvenor Street, London W1X 9PA

LONDON · MELBOURNE
JOHANNESBURG · AUCKLAND

First published 1986
Reprinted 1987
Text © Jean Ure 1986
Illustrations © Glenys Ambrus 1986

A school pack of BANANA BOOKS 13–18 is
available from Heinemann Educational Books
ISBN 0 435 00102 7

434 93037 7
Printed in Hong Kong by
Imago Publishing Ltd

THIS IS THE story of Brenda Bailey, who couldn't say boo to a goose yet came to be known as the most daring girl in the school.

It all began one Monday morning when everybody in the Bailey family, Mr and Mrs Bailey, Brenda and baby Brian (whom Brenda called Brat's Eyes) all woke up late because the alarm clock hadn't gone off. Mr Bailey snatched a quick cup of coffee and went racing down the road to catch his train; Brian (known as Brat's Eyes) screamed in his cot; and Mrs Bailey, still wearing her dressing gown and nightdress, said that Brenda had better go to school on the bus.

'The number 18. You know where to get on and off – and don't forget, if it's crowded, to give up your seat.'

The number 18 bus was full of
people going to work, but not so full
that Brenda couldn't sit down. She sat
downstairs because upstairs there were
all the big children, fighting and
shouting and biffing at each other with
their school bags full of books. Brenda
was scared of the big children. She
was scared of lots of things. At her
primary school they had called her the
Mouse.

After the first stop, two ladies got
on and had to stand. Turning rather
pink (she always turned pink when she
was embarrassed, which actually was
most of the time), Brenda stood up.

Politely, to one of the ladies, she said:
'Would you like my seat?'

The lady looked down at her.

'Why?' she said; and she laughed.
'Do I look as if I'm on my last legs?'
Then she turned to the other lady, and
laughed again, and said: 'Honestly!
They make you feel like a
grandmother.'

Brenda stood for a moment, not sure what to do. Her cheeks had turned so red she felt as if they were on fire. After a bit, when it seemed that the lady was going to go on standing up, she crept back into her seat. She was sure everyone on the bus was looking at her.

Soon another lady got on. She was older than the first ladies. She really *did* look like a grandmother. Brenda stared out of the window as hard as she could. Maybe if she pretended not to notice, somebody else would give the old lady a seat.

Nobody did. When Brenda got off the bus at Park Side Rise, the old lady was still standing there. She gave Brenda quite a cross sort of look. Brenda's cheeks turned red as pillar boxes.

At school, in the playground, she forgot about the old lady. The playground was a sea of children, all playing and shouting and chasing up and down. Brenda stood watching, wishing that she could join in. She had only been at Park Side Juniors a week and was still too shy to talk to anyone.

As she stood there, Michael Patten and Yusuf Patel ran past, their raincoat sleeves tied about their necks, their raincoats flapping behind them like cloaks. They barged into Brenda as they ran, but they didn't stop to say sorry. Michael Patten and Yusuf Patel were part of the great Patten Gang. They were far too grand to take any notice of a new girl.

The other members of the Patten Gang were Jody Barrett and Lorraine Peters. Jody and Lorraine were just nearby. They were jumping up and down and chanting. Brenda looked at them, hopefully. She would have liked to jump up and down and chant. Suddenly, Jody and Lorraine saw her looking at them. They stopped jumping and came over. For a wonderful moment Brenda thought

they were going to ask her if she
would like to jump with them, but all
they did was start dancing in circles
around her, chanting as they went:

      'I'm a chicken,
      You're a duck,
      I lay eggs
      And you lay muck!
      I'm a chicken,
      You're a duck – '

Brenda was glad when the bell rang
for Prayers.

After Prayers they went to their classrooms. Miss Chalk, who was Brenda's class teacher, called the register, then, looking rather stern, she said: 'I have just come from Mrs Marsh.' (Mrs Marsh was the Head Teacher.) 'Someone has made a complaint that one of our pupils, who came to school this morning on the number 18 bus, stayed *sitting down* for several stops while an elderly lady was left to stand.'

An excited murmuring ran round the class: *some*body had been reported. *Some*body was going to get told off. Brenda's face turned slowly pink.

'That pupil,' said Miss Chalk, 'was carrying a bag with her name printed on it. That name – ' she paused, and looked hard at Brenda – 'was Brenda Bailey.'

Thirty pairs of eyes turned in Brenda's direction. A girl called Susan Slater, who was one of Miss Chalk's favourites, let out her breath in a long hiss.

Brenda's cheeks turned cherry red.

'It just so happens,' said Miss Chalk, 'that the elderly lady used to be a pupil here herself once upon a time. She was most upset to think that the pupils of today could have such bad manners.'

Susan Slater pressed her lips together very tightly like a prune. Brenda wanted to curl up and die.

'As you only came to us this term,' said Miss Chalk, 'I will say no more about it. But here at Park Side Juniors we do expect our pupils to give up their seats to older persons. Please remember it another time, Brenda. I shouldn't like to have any more complaints about you. Very well! That's that. Take out your readers.'

As Brenda opened her desk (her cheeks were now the colour of tomato soup) Jody Barrett leaned towards her and whispered: 'That'll be Miss Gibbs, that will. She's always reporting people. She's horrible. We call her Old Toothpaste. Know what she did once?'

'No,' said Brenda.

'I'll tell you,' said Jody; but before she could do so Miss Chalk had rapped on her desk and called, 'Jody Barrett! Stop talking!'

Jody was definitely *not* one of Miss Chalk's favourites. Miss Chalk didn't like any of the Patten Gang. She said they were rude and noisy and trouble-makers. Now, probably, she wouldn't like Brenda either. The Patten Gang didn't worry about Miss Chalk not liking them, because they didn't like Miss Chalk. Brenda worried about it.

She worried all morning. But then at break Yusuf Patel gave her a toffee, which made her feel a bit better, and at dinner time Lorraine Peters made a space for her at table, and after dinner they had drawing, which she was good at, and by the time it came to going home she had almost forgotten about Miss Chalk not liking her.

Up until now, Brenda had always gone home by herself. Today, Jody said: 'Want to walk up the road with us?'

'Might see Old Toothpaste,' said Lorraine. 'Then you could pull faces at her.'

Outside the playground gates Michael and Yusuf were waiting, with their raincoats flapping behind them again like cloaks. Jody nodded towards Brenda. 'She's going to walk up the road with us. OK?'

'OK,' said Michael.

They set off up the road together, the four of them plus Brenda (who was very much hoping that they *didn't* see Miss Gibbs, because if they did she would be so embarrassed she wouldn't know where to look. She would certainly never dare to pull any faces.).

Although Jody had said 'walk', the Patten Gang never walked anywhere when they could run, and they never ran anywhere without shrieking and making a lot of noise (which was just one of the reasons that Miss Chalk didn't like them). As they clattered up Park Side Rise they rattled sticks against the playground railings; and then, when the railings stopped, rattled them against people's fences. Brenda didn't have any stick, and was too timid to shriek, so she just ran.

The High Street was full of people trying to shop. The Gang dodged and ducked and darted in between them, with Brenda hopping along behind and every now and again being given an angry look as one of the others bumped into somebody or sent somebody's bags flying.

Suddenly, with a yell, Michael swooped across the pavement and went charging up a side street. Jody charged with him; so did Yusuf and Lorraine. A lady pushing a pram crossly clicked her tongue and said that she wished people would watch where they were going. Brenda paused just long enough to gasp 'Sorry!' then she, too, went charging off.

She found the others clustered round a tiny cottage which had a big FOR SALE notice outside it. The cottage was very old and crumbly; it looked as if it hadn't been lived in for centuries. The door was closed with a rusty padlock, and all the windows were boarded up. Michael was standing on tiptoe, peering through a gap. As Brenda came puffing round the corner he shouted, 'Look! There's a dead headless body lying on the floor all naked!'

Brenda stopped, in alarm. A dead headless body? *Naked*? The others seemed to like the idea.

'Blood!' screeched Lorraine, pushing Michael out of the way and getting her eye to the crack.

'Look, there's its head!'

'Where? Where? I can't see it!'

'Over there, rolled into the corner –'

'*Ugh! Horrid!*' Jody turned and shouted excitedly at Brenda. 'Come and look!'

Brenda didn't really like the thought of looking at dead naked bodies with their heads rolled into the corner, but even less did she like the thought of Jody and the others knowing what a coward she was. Nervously she crept up to the window and peeped in.

'Can you see it?' cried Jody.

Brenda looked, but she couldn't see anything at all.

'The feet have gone!' shouted Michael. 'It's got no feet!'

'Ugh!'

'Groo!'

'Someone's cut the feet off!'

It took Brenda a moment or so to realise that it was only a game. She was still trying to think of something that *she* could see (a little black dwarf disappearing up the chimney?) when she heard the baby. She was sure it was a baby. She listened again, with her ear to the crack, and it sounded

just like Brat's Eyes. Wheee! wheee!
wheeee! it went, all thin and high. It
was exactly the noise that Brat's Eyes
made when he wanted someone to
cuddle him.

Brenda looked at the others to see if
they had heard, but they were all too
busy shrieking. She knew that she
ought to say something. She opened
her mouth – and then closed it again.
Michael thought that babies were
soppy. Yesterday, in class, when Susan

Slater had told them about her new little sister, Michael had made loud being-sick noises and said, 'Ugh! Babies! *Yuck!*' Miss Chalk had said that he was being very silly and childish, and Susan Slater had said, 'Ugh! Boys! *Yuck!*' and stuck out her tongue.

Brenda knew that she wasn't as brave as Susan Slater. If Michael said 'yuck' to her she would go all red, and anyway it probably wasn't a baby at all, because what would a baby be doing in an empty cottage?

Maybe it was a *stolen* baby. Maybe someone had snatched it from its pram and left it there, and now it was all cold and hungry and frightened at being alone in the dark . . . .

Brenda gulped. She opened her mouth.

'Cc-c-c-can yy-y-y-you hh-h-h-h-h–'

Before she could properly manage to say anything, a man wheeling a wheelbarrow full of cement had come round the corner. He didn't look too pleased to see the Patten Gang and Brenda.

'Come on, you kids!' He jerked his head, impatiently. 'Stop cluttering up the pavement.'

Everybody moved except Michael.

'Why?' said Michael. (He could sometimes be cheeky. That was another reason that Miss Chalk didn't like him.) 'It ain't your pavement.'

The man set down his wheelbarrow.

'No,' he said, 'but this is my hand, and if you don't get a move on you're going to feel the weight of it.'

'Garn!' said Michael.

The man took a step towards him.

'You know what you're asking for,
don't you?' he said. 'You're asking for
a thick ear. Now, scatter – or else!'

With shrieks and giggles, the Gang
scattered. Brenda scattered with them.
In her panic she forgot about the baby,
alone in the empty cottage.

25

Next morning the Baileys' alarm clock went off at the right time and everybody got out of bed when they were supposed to, so that Brenda was able to walk to school as usual. It wasn't until she came to the side street where the cottage was that she remembered about the baby. Could it possibly still be there? Perhaps she ought to go and have just one more listen. Just to make sure.

The baby *was* still there. It was still there, and it was still crying. Wheee . . . wheee . . . wheee . . . it sounded weaker than it had yesterday.

Suddenly, Brenda felt scared. Suppose the baby was starving? Suppose it *died*? She knew that she must be brave and tell someone.

'Excuse me,' she would say, 'but I think there's a baby locked up in this

house.' And then a grown-up would take over and do something and everything would be all right, and Brenda could stop worrying.

A lady was coming out of another cottage two doors up the street.

I must tell the lady, thought Brenda; but as the lady walked past she gave Brenda such a funny look that all Brenda's courage turned to water and started to drip away . . . drip, drip, drip, until there wasn't any left.

The lady went into a shop on the corner. The baby went on crying. Brenda wished that she had never heard it. But she *had* heard it, and if somebody didn't do something then the baby might die.

Perhaps if I went round the back, thought Brenda, I could see something from there.

Round the back was a little garden

all overgrown with great tall purple
thistles and clumps of yellow
dandelions. There was a back door
painted green and two small windows.
Both the windows had been broken,
and the door wasn't quite closed.
Timidly, Brenda pushed at it. To her
surprise it opened; not very far, but
just far enough for her to squeeze
through.

Strangely, she didn't feel scared at being inside the cottage. It smelled a bit musty, as if there might be spiders and other crawly things, but there was sunlight coming through the windows, and outside in the garden, just the other side of the door, were all the purple thistles and the yellow dandelions. In any case, what was more important was that she could now hear the baby crying quite

loudly. It seemed to be coming from somewhere very near – from somewhere in the same *room*. But the room was empty! All there was was an old gas cooker and a sink.

The baby wasn't in the sink. Could someone have put it in the cooker?

Brenda crept forward. She took hold of the handle on the cooker door, and with

thumping heart pulled it open . . .
   The baby wasn't in the cooker.
   The baby wasn't anywhere.
   There wasn't any baby.

What there was was an old, old fan, high up near the ceiling. The fan was going round, all by itself. Round and round it was going. And as it went round it went wheee, wheee, wheee . . . just like a baby.

Brenda had never felt so foolish in all her life. Thank goodness she hadn't told anyone! If Michael knew, he would laugh until he was sick.

Michael mustn't ever know. *Nobody* must know.

Brenda began squeezing herself out again through the narrow gap in the doorway. First she squeezed a leg, and then she squeezed an arm; and after that a shoulder, and then, very carefully, the rest of her. It was just as her head was coming out into the sunlight, into the garden with the dandelions and thistles, that a hand suddenly clamped on to her wrist and a triumphant voice cried: 'Got you! You young vandal!'

It was the lady who had come out of the cottage two doors up and given her the funny look . . . .

At school next day Miss Chalk was terribly and terrifically cross.

'Really, Brenda!' she said. She said it in front of the whole class. 'Whatever next? Breaking into other people's property like that! You surely must have known that it was wrong?'

Susan Slater, sitting in the front row, said: 'Trespassers will be Prosecuted.'

'Being prosecuted means being taken to court,' said Miss Chalk. (Brenda trembled slightly. Only *really* bad children were taken to court.) 'That won't happen to Brenda, because she didn't do any damage – but that's still no excuse for being so naughty! I can see, Brenda, that in future I am going to have to keep my eye on you. You are obviously going to be a Trouble-Maker.'

Afterwards, at break, the Gang gathered round.

'You mean, you went *in* there?' said Michael.

'*Right* in?' said Yusuf.

'By your*self*?' said Lorraine.

'You know that it's haunted,' said Jody, 'don't you?'

'H-haunted?' said Brenda.

'Yes, by a headless ghost that drips blood.'

'And everyone that goes in there gets turned into jelly.'

'J-jelly?' said Brenda.

Now that she came to think about it, her legs *were* feeling a bit jelly-like.

'It makes this noise,' said Yusuf, 'to warn people not to go in.'

'Yes, and if you hear the noise,' said Jody, 'that's when you're done for.'

'That's when you get turned into jelly.'

Brenda swallowed. Her legs, quite definitely, were starting to wobble.

'It's hearing the noise,' said Michael, 'that's the most dangerous of all.'

'W-what s-s-s – ' (now her voice was starting to wobble as well) 'what s-sort of n-noise?'

'A horrible noise.'

'Like this,' said Yusuf. He put his hands round his mouth. 'Wheee . . . wheee . . . wheee. . . .'

He sounded just like a baby crying. (Or like a fan going round, all by itself.)

'Turns you to jelly,' said Lorraine.

'Takes about an hour,' said Jody. 'About an hour after you've been in there.'

'All your bones go melty,' said Yusuf.

They looked at her.

'Are your bones going melty?' said
Jody.

'Not yet,' said Brenda. It was
funny, but the jelly-like feeling had
quite gone.

'P'raps that's 'cos you didn't hear
the noise,' said Jody.

'I did,' said Brenda.

'You *did*?'

They stared at her, big-eyed.

'Aren't you scared?' said Michael.

Brenda thought about it.

'Not really,' she said.

There was a silence.

'Cor!' said Jody.